THE TOWER OF THE ELEPHANT

BY

ROBERT E. HOWARD

British Library Cataloguing-in-Publication Data
A catalogue record for this book is available from the
British Library

Contents

Robert E. Howard

Robert Ervin Howard was born in Peaster, Texas in 1906. During his youth, his family moved between a variety of Texan boomtowns, and Howard – a bookish and somewhat introverted child – was steeped in the violent myths and legends of the Old South. Although he loved reading and learning, Howard developed a distinctly Texan, hardboiled outlook on the world. He became a passionate fan of boxing, taking it up at an amateur level, and from the age of nine began to write adventure tales of semi-historical bloodshed. In 1919, when Howard was thirteen, his family moved to the Central Texas hamlet of Cross Plains, where he would stay for the rest of his life.

At fifteen Howard began to read the pulp magazines of the day, and to write more seriously. The December 1922 issue of his high school newspaper featured two of his stories, 'Golden Hope Christmas' and 'West is West'. In 1924 he sold his first piece – a short caveman tale titled 'Spear and Fang' – for $16 to the not-yet-famous *Weird Tales* magazine. He published with the magazine regularly over the next few years. 1929 was a breakout year for Howard, in that the 23-year-old writer began to sell to other magazines, such as *Ghost Stories* and *Argosy*, both of whom had previously sent him hundreds of rejection slips. In 1930, he began a correspondence with weird fiction master H. P. Lovecraft which ran up to his death six years later, and is regarded as one of the great correspondence cycles in all of fantasy literature.

It was partly due to Lovecraft's encouragement that Howard created his most famous character, Conan the Cimmerian. Conan – a barbarian-turned-King during the Hyborian Age, a mythical period of some 12,000 years ago – featured in seventeen *Weird Tales* stories between 1933 and 1936, and is now regarded as having spawned the 'sword and sorcery' genre, making Howard's influence on fantasy literature comparable to that of J. R. R. Tolkien's. The Conan stories have since been adapted many times, most famously in the series of films starring Arnold Schwarzenegger.

Howard was enjoying an all-time high in sales by the beginning of 1936, but he was also deeply upset by the ill health of his mother, who had fallen into a coma. On the morning of June 11, 1936, he asked an attending nurse whether she would ever recover, and the nurse replied negatively. Howard walked to his car, parked outside the family home in Cross Plains, and shot himself. He died eight hours later, aged just thirty.

CHAPTER I

Torches flared murkily on the revels in the Maul, where the thieves of the east held carnival by night. In the Maul they could carouse and roar as they liked, for honest people shunned the quarters, and watchmen, well paid with stained coins, did not interfere with their sport. Along the crooked, unpaved streets with their heaps of refuse and sloppy puddles, drunken roisterers staggered, roaring. Steel glinted in the shadows where wolf preyed on wolf, and from the darkness rose the shrill laughter of women, and the sounds of scufflings and strugglings. Torchlight licked luridly from broken windows and wide-thrown doors, and out of those doors, stale smells of wine and rank sweaty bodies, clamor of drinking-jacks and fists hammered on rough tables, snatches of obscene songs, rushed like a blow in the face.

In one of these dens merriment thundered to the low smoke-stained roof, where rascals gathered in every stage of rags and tatters—furtive cut-purses, leering kidnappers, quick-fingered thieves, swaggering bravoes with their wenches, strident-voiced women clad in tawdry finery. Native rogues were the dominant element—dark-skinned, dark-eyed Zamorians, with daggers at their girdles and guile in their hearts. But there were wolves of half a dozen outland nations there as well. There was a giant Hyperborean renegade, taciturn, dangerous, with a broadsword strapped to his great gaunt frame—for men wore steel openly in the Maul. There was a Shemitish counterfeiter, with his hook nose and curled blue black beard. There was a bold-eyed Brythunian wench, sitting on the knee of a tawny-haired Gunderman—a wandering mercenary soldier, a deserter from some defeated army. And the fat gross rogue whose bawdy jests were causing all the shouts of mirth was a professional kidnapper come up from distant Koth to teach woman-stealing to Zamorians who were born with more knowledge of the art than he could ever attain.

This man halted in his description of an intended victim's charms, and thrust his muzzle into a huge tankard of frothing ale. Then blowing-the foam from his fat lips, he said, "By Bel, god of all thieves, I'll show them how to steal wenches: I'll have her over the Zamorian border before dawn, and there'll be a caravan waiting to receive her. Three hundred pieces of silver, a count of Ophir promised me for a sleek young Brythunian of the better class. It took me weeks, wandering among the border cities as a beggar, to find one I knew would suit. And is she a pretty baggage!"

He blew a slobbery kiss in the air.

"I know lords in Shem who would trade the secret of the Elephant Tower for her," he said, returning to his ale.

A touch on his tunic sleeve made him turn his head, scowling at the interruption. He saw a tall, strongly made youth standing beside him. This person was as much out of place in that den as a gray wolf among mangy rats of the gutters. His cheap tunic could not conceal the hard, rangy lines of his powerful frame, the broad heavy shoulders, the massive chest, lean waist, and heavy arms. His skin was brown from outland suns, his eyes blue and smoldering; a shock of tousled black hair crowned his broad forehead. From his girdle hung a sword in a worn leather scabbard.

The Kothian involuntarily drew back; for the man was not one of any civilized race he knew.

"You spoke of the Elephant Tower," said the stranger, speaking Zamorian with an alien accent. "I've heard much of this tower; what is its secret?"

The fellow's attitude did not seem threatening, and the Kothian's courage was bolstered up by the ale, and the evident approval of his audience. He swelled with self-importance.

"The secret of the Elephant Tower?" he exclaimed. "Why, any fool knows that Yara the priest dwells there with the great jewel men call the Elephant's Heart, that is the secret of his magic."

The barbarian digested this for a space.

"I have seen this tower," he said. "It is set in a great garden above the level of the city, surrounded by high walls. I have seen no guards. The walls would be easy to climb. Why has not somebody stolen this secret gem?"

The Kothian stared wide-mouthed at the other's simplicity, then burst into a roar of derisive mirth, in which the others joined.

"Harken to this heathen!" he bellowed. "He would steal the jewel of Yara!   Harken, fellow," he said, turning portentously to the other, "I suppose you are some sort of a northern barbarian—"

"I am a Cimmerian," the outlander answered, in no friendly tone. The reply and the manner of it meant little to the Kothian; of a kingdom that lay far to the south, on the borders of Shem, he knew only vaguely of the northern races.

"Then give ear and learn wisdom, fellow," said he, pointing his drinking-jack at the discomfited youth. "Know that in Zamora, and more especially in this city, there are more bold thieves than anywhere else in the world, even Koth. If mortal man could have stolen the gem, be sure it would have been filched long ago. You speak of climbing the walls, but once having climbed, you would quickly wish yourself back again. There are no guards in the gardens at night for a very good reason—that is, no human guards. But in the watch-chamber, in the lower part of the tower, are armed men, and even if you passed those who roam the gardens by night, you must still pass through the soldiers, for the gem is kept somewhere in the tower above."

"But if a man could pass through the gardens," argued the Cimmerian, "why could he not come at the gem through the upper part of the tower and thus avoid the soldiers?"

Again the Kothian gaped at him.

"Listen to him!" he shouted jeeringly. "The barbarian is an eagle who would fly to the jeweled rim of the tower, which is only a hundred and fifty feet above the earth, with rounded sides slicker than polished glass!"

The Cimmerian glared about, embarrassed at the roar of mocking laughter that greeted this remark. He saw no particular humor in it, and was too new to civilization to understand its discourtesies. Civilized men are more discourteous than savages because they know they can be impolite without having their skulls split, as a general thing. He was bewildered and chagrined, and doubtless would have slunk away, abashed, but the Kothian chose to goad him further.

"Come, come!" he shouted. "Tell these poor fellows, who have only been thieves since before you were spawned, tell them how you would steal the gem!"

"There is always a way, if the desire be coupled with courage," answered the Cimmerian shortly, nettled.

The Kothian chose to take this as a personal slur. His face grew purple with anger.

"What!" he roared. "You dare tell us our business, and intimate that we are cowards? Get along; get out of my sight!" And he pushed the Cimmerian violently.

"Will you mock me and then lay hands on me?" grated the barbarian, his quick rage leaping up; and he returned the push with an open-handed blow that knocked his tormenter back against the rude-hewn table. Ale splashed over the jack's lip, and the Kothian roared in fury, dragging at his sword.

"Heathen dog!" he bellowed. "I'll have your heart for that!"

Steel flashed and the throng surged wildly back out of the way. In their flight they knocked over the single candle and the den was plunged in darkness, broken by the crash of upset benches, drum of flying feet, shouts, oaths of people tumbling over one another, and a single strident yell of agony that cut the din like a knife. When a candle was relighted, most of the guests had gone out by doors and broken windows, and the rest huddled behind stacks of wine-kegs and under tables. The barbarian was gone; the center of the room was deserted except for the gashed body of the Kothian. The Cimmerian, with the unerring instinct of the barbarian, had killed his man in the darkness and confusion.

CHAPTER II

The lurid lights and drunken revelry fell away behind the Cimmerian. He had discarded his torn tunic, and walked through the night naked except for a loin-cloth and his high-strapped sandals. He moved with the supple ease of a great tiger, his steely muscles rippling under his brown skin.

He had entered the part of the city reserved for the temples. On all sides of him they glittered white in the starlight—snowy marble pillars and golden domes and silver arches, shrines of Zamora's myriad strange gods. He did not trouble his head about them; he knew that Zamora's religion, like all things of a civilized, long settled people, was intricate and complex, and had lost most of the pristine essence in a maze of formulas and rituals. He had squatted for hours in the courtyards of the philosophers, listening to the arguments of theologians and teachers, and come away in a haze of bewilderment, sure of only one thing, and that, that they were all touched in the head.

His gods were simple and understandable; Crom was their chief, and he lived on a great mountain, whence he sent forth dooms and death. It was useless to call on Crom, because he was a gloomy, savage god, and he hated weaklings. But he gave a man courage at birth, and the will and might to kill his enemies, which, in the Cimmerian's mind, was all any god should be expected to do.

His sandalled feet made no sound on the gleaming pave. No watchmen passed, for even the thieves of the Maul shunned the temples, where strange dooms had been known to fall on violators. Ahead of him he saw, looming against the sky, the Tower of the Elephant. He mused, wondering why it was so named. No one seemed to know. He had never seen an elephant, but he vaguely understood that it was a monstrous animal, with a tail in front as well as behind. This a wandering Shemite had told him, swearing that he had seen such beasts by the thousands in the country of the Hyrkanians; but all men knew what liars were the men of Shem. At any rate, there were no elephants in Zamora.

The shimmering shaft of the tower rose frostily in the stars. In the sunlight it shone so dazzlingly that few could bear its glare, and men said it was built of silver. It was round, a slim perfect cylinder, a hundred and fifty feet in height, and its rim glittered in the starlight with the great jewels which crusted it. The tower stood among the waving exotic trees of a garden raised high above the general level of the city. A high wall enclosed this garden, and outside the wall was a lower level, likewise enclosed by a wall. No lights shone forth; there seemed to be no windows in the tower—at least not above the level of the inner wall. Only the gems high above sparkled frostily in the starlight.

Shrubbery grew thick outside the lower, or outer wall. The Cimmerian crept close and stood beside the barrier, measuring it with his eye. It was high, but he could leap and catch the coping with his fingers. Then it would be child's play to swing himself up and over, and he did not doubt that he could pass the inner wall in the same manner. But he hesitated at the thought of the strange perils which were said to await within. These people were strange and mysterious to him; they were not of his kind—not even of the same blood as the more westerly Brythunians, Nemedians, Kothians and Aquilonians, whose civilized mysteries had awed him in times past. The people of Zamora were very ancient, and, from what he had seen of them, very evil.

He thought of Yara, the high priest, who worked strange dooms from this jeweled tower, and the Cimmerian's hair prickled as he remembered a tale told by a drunken page of the court—how Yara had laughed in the face of a hostile prince, and held up a glowing, evil gem before him, and how rays shot blindingly from that unholy jewel, to envelop the prince, who screamed and fell down, and shrank to a withered blackened lump that changed to a black spider which scampered wildly about the chamber until Yara set his heel upon it.

Yara came not often from his tower of magic, and always to work evil on some man or some nation. The king of Zamora feared him more than he feared death, and kept himself drunk all the time because that fear was more than he could endure sober. Yara was very old—centuries old, men said, and added that he would live for ever because of the magic of his gem, which men called the Heart of the Elephant, for no better reason than they named his hold the Elephant's Tower.

The Cimmerian, engrossed in these thoughts, shrank quickly against the wall. Within the garden some one was passing, who walked with a measured stride. The listener heard the clink of steel. So after all a guard did pace those gardens. The Cimmerian waited, expected to hear him pass again, on the next round, but silence rested over the mysterious gardens.

At last curiosity overcame him. Leaping lightly he grasped the wall and swung himself up to the top with one arm. Lying flat on the broad coping, he looked down into the wide space between the walls. No shrubbery grew near him, though he saw some carefully trimmed bushes near the inner wall. The starlight fell on the even sward and somewhere a fountain tinkled.

The Cimmerian cautiously lowered himself down on the inside and drew his sword, staring about him. He was shaken by the nervousness of the wild at standing thus unprotected in the naked starlight, and he moved lightly around the curve of the wall, hugging its shadow, until he was even with the shrubbery he had noticed. Then he ran quickly toward it, crouching low, and almost tripped over a form that lay crumpled near the edges of the bushes.

A quick look to right and left showed him no enemy in sight at least, and he bent close to investigate. His keen eyes, even in the dim starlight, showed him a strongly built man in the silvered armor and crested helmet of the Zamorian royal guard. A shield and a spear lay near him, and it took but an instant's examination to show that he had been strangled. The barbarian glanced about uneasily. He knew that this man must be the guard he had heard pass his hiding-place by the wall. Only a short time had passed, yet in that interval nameless hands had reached out of the dark and choked out the soldier's life.

Straining his eyes in the gloom, he saw a hint of motion through the shrubs near the wall. Thither he glided, gripping his sword. He made no more noise than a panther stealing through the night, yet the man he was stalking heard. The Cimmerian had a dim glimpse of a huge bulk close to the wall, felt relief that it was at least human; then the fellow wheeled quickly with a gasp that sounded like panic, made the first motion of a forward plunge, hands clutching, then recoiled as the Cimmerian's blade caught the starlight. For a tense instant neither spoke, standing ready for anything.

"You are no soldier," hissed the stranger at last. "You are a thief like myself"

"And who are you?" asked the Cimmerian in a suspicious whisper.

"Taurus of Nemedia."

The Cimmerian lowered his sword.

"I've heard of you. Men call you a prince of thieves."

A low laugh answered him. Taurus was tall as the Cimmerian, and heavier; he was big-bellied and fat, but his every movement betokened a subtle dynamic magnetism, which was reflected in the keen eyes that glinted vitally, even in the starlight. He was barefooted and carried a coil of what looked like a thin, strong rope, knotted at regular intervals.

"Who are you?" he whispered.

"Conan, a Cimmerian," answered the other. "I came seeking a way to steal Yara's jewel, that men call the Elephant's Heart."

Conan sensed the man's great belly shaking in laughter, but it was not derisive. "By Bel, god of thieves!" hissed Taurus. "I had thought only myself had courage to attempt that poaching. These Zamorians call themselves thieves—bah! Conan, I like your grit. I never shared an adventure with anyone, but by Bel, we'll attempt this together if you're willing."

"Then you are after the gem, too?"

"What else? I've had my plans laid for months, but you, I think, have acted on sudden impulse, my friend."

"You killed the soldier?"

"Of course. I slid over the wall when he was on the other side of the garden. I hid in the bushes; he heard me, or thought he heard something. When he came blundering over, it was no trick at all to get behind him and suddenly grip his neck and choke out his fool's life. He was like most men, half blind in the dark. A good thief should have eyes like a cat."

"You made one mistake," said Conan.

Taurus' eyes flashed angrily.

"I? I, a mistake? Impossible!"

"You should have dragged the body into the bushes."

"Said the novice to the master of the art. They will not change the guard until past midnight. Should any come searching for him now, and find his body, they would flee at once to Yara, bellowing the news, and give us time to escape. Were they not to find it, they'd go beating up the bushes and catch us like rats in a trap."

"You are right," agreed Conan.

"So. Now attend. We waste time in this cursed discussion. There are no guards in the inner garden—human guards, I mean, though there are sentinels even more deadly. It was their presence which baffled me for so long, but I finally discovered a way to circumvent them."

"What of the soldiers in the lower part of the tower?"

"Old Yara dwells in the chambers above. By that route we will come—and go, I hope. Never mind asking me how.

I have arranged a way. We'll steal down through the top of the tower and strangle old Yara before he can cast any of his accursed spells on us. At least we'll try; it's the chance of being turned into a spider or a toad, against the wealth and power of the world. All good thieves must know how to take risks."

"I'll go as far as any man," said Conan, slipping off his sandals.

"Then follow me." And turning, Taurus leaped up, caught the wall and drew himself up. The man's suppleness was amazing, considering his bulk; he seemed almost to glide up over the edge of the coping. Conan followed him, and lying flat on the broad top, they spoke in wary whispers.

"I see no light," Conan muttered. The lower part of the tower seemed much like that portion visible from outside the garden—a perfect, gleaming cylinder, with no apparent openings.

"There are cleverly constructed doors and windows," answered Taurus, "but they are closed. The soldiers breathe air that comes from above."

The garden was a vague pool of shadows, where feathery bushes and low spreading trees waved darkly in the starlight. Conan's wary soul felt the aura of waiting menace that brooded over it. He felt the burning glare of unseen eyes, and he caught a subtle scent that made the short hairs on his neck instinctively bristle as a hunting dog bristles at the scent of an ancient enemy.

"Follow me," whispered Taurus, "keep behind me, as you value your life."

Taking what looked like a copper tube from his girdle, the Nemedian dropped lightly to the sward inside the wall. Conan was close behind him, sword ready, but Taurus pushed him back, close to the wall, and showed no inclination to advance, himself. His whole attitude was of tense expectancy, and his gaze, like Conan's, was fixed on the shadowy mass of shrubbery a few yards away. This shrubbery was shaken, although the breeze had died down. Then two great eyes blazed from the waving shadows, and behind them other sparks of fire glinted in the darkness.

"Lions!" muttered Conan.

"Aye. By day they are kept in subterranean caverns below the tower. That's why there are no guards in this garden."

Conan counted the eyes rapidly.

"Five in sight; maybe more back in the bushes. They'll charge in a moment—"

"Be silent!" hissed Taurus, and he moved out from the wall, cautiously as if treading on razors, lifting the slender tube. Low rumblings rose from the shadows and the blazing eyes moved forward. Conan could sense the great slavering jaws, the tufted tails lashing tawny sides. The air grew tense—the Cimmerian gripped his sword, expecting the charge and the irresistible hurtling of giant bodies. Then Taurus brought the mouth of the tube to his lips and blew powerfully. A long jet of yellowish powder shot from the other end of the tube and billowed out instantly in a thick green-yellow cloud that settled over the shrubbery, blotting out the glaring eyes.

Taurus ran back hastily to the wall. Conan glared without understanding. The thick cloud hid the shrubbery, and from it no sound came.

"What is that mist?" the Cimmerian asked uneasily.

"Death!" hissed the Nemedian. "If a wind springs up and blows it back upon us, we must flee over the wall. But no, the wind is still, and now it is dissipating. Wait until it vanishes entirely. To breathe it is death."

Presently only yellowish shreds hung ghostily in the air; then they were gone, and Taurus motioned his companion forward. They stole toward the bushes, and Conan gasped. Stretched out in the shadows lay five great tawny shapes, the fire of their grim eyes dimmed for ever. A sweetish cloying scent lingered in the atmosphere.

"They died without a sound!" muttered the Cimmerian. "Taurus, what was that powder?"

"It was made from the black lotus, whose blossoms wave in the lost jungles of Khitai, where only the yellow-skulled priests of Yun dwell. Those blossoms strike dead any who smell of them."

Conan knelt beside the great forms, assuring himself that they were indeed beyond power of harm. He shook his head; the magic of the exotic lands was mysterious and terrible to the barbarians of the north.

"Why can you not slay the soldiers in the tower in the same way?" he asked.

"Because that was all the powder I possessed. The obtaining of it was a feat which in itself was enough to make me famous among the thieves of the world. I stole it out of a caravan bound for Stygia, and I lifted it, in its cloth-of-gold bag, out of the coils of the great serpent which guarded it, without awaking him. But come, in Bel's name! Are we to waste the night in discussion?"

They glided through the shrubbery to the gleaming foot of the tower, and there, with a motion enjoining silence, Taurus unwound his knotted cord, on one end of which was a strong steel hook. Conan saw his plan, and asked no questions as the Nemedian gripped the line a short distance below the hook, and began to swing it about his head. Conan laid his ear to the smooth wall and listened, but could hear nothing. Evidently the soldiers within did not suspect the presence of intruders, who had made no more sound than the night wind blowing through the trees. But a strange nervousness was on the barbarian; perhaps it was the lion-smell which was over everything.

Taurus threw the line with a smooth, ripping motion of his mighty arm. The hook curved upward and inward in a peculiar manner, hard to describe, and vanished over the jeweled rim. It apparently caught firmly, for cautious jerking and then hard pulling did not result in any slipping or giving.

"Luck the first cast," murmured Taurus. "I—"

It was Conan's savage instinct which made him wheel suddenly; for the death that was upon them made no sound. A fleeting glimpse showed the Cimmerian the giant tawny shape, rearing upright against the stars, towering over him for the death-stroke. No civilized man could have moved half so quickly as the barbarian moved. His sword flashed frostily in the starlight with every ounce of desperate nerve and thew behind it, and man and beast went down together.

Cursing incoherently beneath his breath, Taurus bent above the mass, and saw his companion's limbs move as he strove to drag himself from under the great weight that lay limply upon him. A glance showed the startled Nemedian that the lion was dead, its slanting skull split in half. He laid hold of the carcass, and by his aid, Conan thrust it aside and clambered up, still gripping his dripping sword.

"Are you hurt, man?" gasped Taurus, still bewildered by the stunning swiftness of that touch-and-go episode.

"No, by Crom!" answered the barbarian. "But that was as close a call as I've had in a life noways tame. Why did not the cursed beast roar as he charged?"

"All things are strange in this garden," said Taurus. "The lions strike silently—and so do other deaths. But come— little sound was made in that slaying, but the soldiers might have heard, if they are not asleep or drunk. That beast was in some other part of the garden and escaped the death of the flowers, but surely there are no more. We must climb this cord—little need to ask a Cimmerian if he can."

"If it will bear my weight," grunted Conan, cleansing his sword on the grass. "It will bear thrice my own," answered Taurus. "It was woven from the tresses of dead women, which I took from their tombs at midnight, and steeped in the deadly wine of the upas tree, to give it strength. I will go first—then follow me closely."

The Nemedian gripped the rope and crooking a knee about it, began the ascent; he went up like a cat, belying the apparent clumsiness of his bulk. The Cimmerian followed. The cord swayed and turned on itself, but the climbers were not hindered; both had made more difficult climbs before. The jeweled rim glittered high above them, jutting out from the perpendicular of the wall, so that the cord hung perhaps a foot from the side of the tower—a fact which added greatly to the ease of the ascent.

Up and up they went, silently, the lights of the city spreading out further and further to their sight as they climbed, the stars above them more and more dimmed by the glitter of the jewels along the rim. Now Taurus reached up a hand and gripped the rim itself, pulling himself up and over. Conan paused a moment on the very edge, fascinated by the great frosty jewels whose gleams dazzled his eyes—diamonds, rubies, emeralds, sapphires, turquoises, moonstones, set thick as stars in the shimmering silver. At a distance their different gleams had seemed to merge into a pulsing white glare; but now, at close range, they shimmered with a million rainbow tints and lights, hypnotizing him with their scintillations.

"There is a fabulous fortune here, Taurus," he whispered; but the Nemedian answered impatiently, "Come on! If we secure the Heart, these and all other things shall be ours."

Conan climbed over the sparkling rim. The level of the tower's top was some feet below the gemmed ledge. It was flat, composed of some dark blue substance, set with gold that caught the starlight, so that the whole looked like a wide sapphire flecked with shining gold-dust. Across from the point where they had entered there seemed to be a sort of chamber, built upon the roof. It was of the same silvery material as the walls of the tower, adorned with designs worked in smaller gems; its single door was of gold, its surface cut in scales, and crusted with jewels that gleamed like ice.

Conan cast a glance at the pulsing ocean of lights which spread far below them, then glanced at Taurus. The Nemedian was drawing up his cord and coiling it. He showed Conan where the hook had caught—a fraction of an inch of the point had sunk under a great blazing jewel on the inner side of the rim.

"Luck was with us again," he muttered. "One would think that our combined weight would have torn that stone out. Follow me; the real risks of the venture begin now. We are in the serpent's lair, and we know not where he lies hidden."

Like stalking tigers they crept across the darkly gleaming floor and halted outside the sparkling door. With a deft and cautious hand Taurus tried it. It gave without resistance, and the companions looked in, tensed for anything. Over the Nemedian's shoulder Conan had a glimpse of a glittering chamber, the walls, ceiling and floor of which were crusted with great white jewels which lighted it brightly, and which seemed its only illumination. It seemed empty of life.

"Before we cut off our last retreat," hissed Taurus, "go you to the rim and look over on all sides; if you see any soldiers moving in the gardens, or anything suspicious, return and tell me. I will await you within this chamber."

Conan saw scant reason in this, and a faint suspicion of his companion touched his wary soul, but he did as Taurus requested. As he turned away, the Nemedian slipt inside the door and drew it shut behind him. Conan crept about the rim of the tower, returning to his starting-point without having seen any suspicious movement in the vaguely waving sea of leaves below. He turned toward the door-suddenly from within the chamber there sounded a strangled cry.

The Cimmerian leaped forward, electrified—the gleaming door swung open and Taurus stood framed in the cold blaze behind him. He swayed and his lips parted, but only a dry rattle burst from his throat. Catching at the golden door for support, he lurched out upon the roof, then fell headlong, clutching at his throat. The door swung to behind him.

Conan, crouching like a panther at bay, saw nothing in the room behind the stricken Nemedian, in the brief instant the door was partly open—unless it was not a trick of the light which made it seem as if a shadow darted across the gleaming floor. Nothing followed Taurus out on the roof, and Conan bent above the man.

The Nemedian stared up with dilated, glazing eyes, that somehow held a terrible bewilderment. His hands clawed at his throat, his lips slobbered and gurgled; then suddenly he stiffened, and the astounded Cimmerian knew that he was dead. And he felt that Taurus had died without knowing what manner of death had stricken him. Conan glared bewilderedly at the cryptic golden door. In that empty room, with its glittering jeweled walls, death had come to the prince of thieves as swiftly and mysteriously as he had dealt doom to the lions in the gardens below.

Gingerly the barbarian ran his hands over the man's half-naked body, seeking a wound. But the only marks of violence were between his shoulders, high up near the base of his bull-neck—three small wounds, which looked as if three nails had been driven deep in the flesh and withdrawn. The edges of these wounds were black, and a faint smell as of putrefaction was evident. Poisoned darts? thought Conan— but in that case the missiles should be still in the wounds.

Cautiously he stole toward the golden door, pushed it open, and looked inside. The chamber lay empty, bathed in the cold, pulsing glow of the myriad jewels. In the very center of the ceiling he idly noted a curious design—a black eight-sided pattern, in the center of which four gems glittered with a red flame unlike the white blaze of the other jewels. Across the room there was another door, like the one in which he stood, except that it was not carved in the scale pattern. Was it from that door that death had come?—and having struck down its victim, had it retreated by the same way?

Closing the door behind him, the Cimmerian advanced into the chamber. His bare feet made no sound on the crystal floor. There were no chairs or tables in the chamber, only three or four silken couches, embroidered with gold and worked in strange serpentine designs, and several silver-bound mahogany chests. Some were sealed with heavy golden locks; others lay open, their carven lids thrown back, revealing heaps of jewels in a careless riot of splendor to the Cimmerian's astounded eyes. Conan swore beneath his breath; already he had looked upon more wealth that night than he had ever dreamed existed in all the world, and he grew dizzy thinking of what must be the value of the jewel he sought.

He was in the center of the room now, going stooped forward, head thrust out warily, sword advanced, when again death struck at him soundlessly. A flying shadow that swept across the gleaming floor was his only warning, and his instinctive sidelong leap all that saved his life. He had a flashing glimpse of a hairy black horror that swung past him with a clashing of frothing fangs, and something splashed on his bare shoulder that burned like drops of liquid hell-fire. Springing back, sword high, he saw the horror strike the floor, wheel and scuttle toward him with appalling speed—a gigantic black spider, such as men see only in nightmare dreams.

It was as large as a pig, and its eight thick hairy legs drove its ogreish body over the floor at headlong pace; its four evilly gleaming eyes shone with a horrible intelligence, and its fangs dripped venom that Conan knew, from the burning of his shoulder where only a few drops had splashed as the thing struck and missed, was laden with swift death. This was the killer that had dropped from its perch in the middle of the ceiling on a strand of its web, on the neck of the Nemedian. Fools that they were not to have suspected that the upper chambers would be guarded as well as the lower!

These thoughts flashed briefly through Conan's mind as the monster rushed. He leaped high, and it passed beneath him, wheeled and charged back. This time he evaded its rush with a sidewise leap, and struck back like a cat. His sword severed one of the hairy legs, and again he barely saved himself as the monstrosity swerved at him, fangs clicking fiendishly. But the creature did not press the pursuit; turning, it scuttled across the crystal floor and ran up the wall to the ceiling, where it crouched for an instant, glaring down at him with its fiendish red eyes. Then without warning it launched itself through space, trailing a strand of slimy grayish stuff.

Conan stepped back to avoid the hurtling body—then ducked frantically, just in time to escape being snared by the flying web-rope. He saw the monster's intent and sprang toward the door, but it was quicker, and a sticky strand cast across the door made him a prisoner. He dared not try to cut it with his sword; he knew the stuff would cling to the blade, and before he could shake it loose, the fiend would be sinking its fangs in to his back.

Then began a desperate game, the wits and quickness of the man matched against the fiendish craft and speed of the giant spider. It no longer scuttled across the floor in a direct charge, or swung its body through the air at him. It raced about the ceiling and the walls, seeking to snare him in the long loops of sticky gray web strands, which it flung with a devilish accuracy. These strands were thick as ropes, and Conan knew that once they were coiled about him, his desperate strength would not be enough to tear him free before the monster struck.

All over the chamber went on that devil's dance, in utter silence except for the quick breathing of the man, the low scuff of his bare feet on the shining floor, the castanet rattle of the monstrosity's fangs. The gray strands lay in coils on the floor; they were looped along the walls; they overlaid the jewel-chests and silken couches, and hung in dusky festoons from the jeweled ceiling. Conan's steel-trap quickness of eye and muscle had kept him untouched, though the sticky loops had passed him so close they rasped his naked hide. He knew he could not always avoid them; he not only had to watch the strands swinging from the ceiling, but to keep his eye on the floor, lest he trip in the coils that lay there. Sooner or later a gummy loop would writhe about him, python-like, and then, wrapped like a cocoon, he would lie at the monster's mercy.

The spider raced across the chamber floor, the gray rope waving out behind it. Conan leaped high, clearing a couch—with a quick wheel the fiend ran up the wall, and the strand, leaping off the floor like a live thing, whipped about the Cimmerian's ankle. He caught himself on his hands as he fell, jerking frantically at the web which held him like a pliant vise, or the coil of a python. The hairy devil was racing down the wall to complete its capture. Stung to frenzy, Conan caught up a jewel chest and hurled it with all his strength. It was a move the monster was not expecting. Full in the midst of the branching black legs the massive missile struck, smashing against the wall with a muffled sickening crunch. Blood and greenish slime spattered, and the shattered mass fell with the burst gem-chest to the floor. The crushed black body lay among the flaming riot of jewels that spilled over it; the hairy legs moved aimlessly, the dying eyes glittered redly among the twinkling gems.

Conan glared about, but no other horror appeared, and he set himself to working free of the web. The substance clung tenaciously to his ankle and his hands, but at last he was free, and taking up his sword, he picked his way among the gray coils and loops to the inner door. What horrors lay within he did not know. The Cimmerian's blood was up, and since he had come so far, and overcome so much peril, he was determined to go through to the grim finish of the adventure, whatever that might be. And he felt that the jewel he sought was not among the many so carelessly strewn about the gleaming chamber.

Stripping off the loops that fouled the inner door, he found that it, like the other, was not locked. He wondered if the soldiers below were still unaware of his presence. Well, he was high above their heads, and if tales were to be believed, they were used to strange noises in the tower above them—sinister sounds, and screams of agony and horror.

Yara was on his mind, and he was not altogether comfortable as he opened the golden door. But he saw only a flight of silver steps leading down, dimly lighted by what means he could not ascertain. Down these he went silently, gripping his sword. He heard no sound, and came presently to an ivory door, set with blood stones. He listened, but no sound came from within; only thin wisps of smoke drifted lazily from beneath the door, bearing a curious exotic odor unfamiliar to the Cimmerian. Below him the silver stair wound down to vanish in the dimness, and up that shadowy well no sound floated; he had an eery feeling that he was alone in a tower occupied only by ghosts and phantoms.

CHAPTER III

Cautiously he pressed against the ivory door and it swung silently inward. On the shimmering threshold Conan stared like a wolf in strange surroundings, ready to fight or flee on the instant. He was looking into a large chamber with a domed golden ceiling; the walls were of green jade, the floor of ivory, partly covered by thick rugs. Smoke and exotic scent of incense floated up from a brazier on a golden tripod, and behind it sat an idol on a sort of marble couch. Conan stared aghast; the image had the body of a man, naked, and green in color; but the head was one of nightmare and madness. Too large for the human body, it had no attributes of humanity. Conan stared at the wide flaring ears, the curling proboscis, on either side of which stood white tusks tipped with round golden balls. The eyes were closed, as if in sleep.

This then, was the reason for the name, the Tower of the Elephant, for the head of the thing was much like that of the beasts described by the Shemitish wanderer. This was Yara's god; where then should the gem be, but concealed in the idol, since the stone was called the Elephant's Heart?

As Conan came forward, his eyes fixed on the motionless idol, the eyes of the thing opened suddenly! The Cimmerian froze in his tracks. It was no image—it was a living thing, and he was trapped in its chamber!

That he did not instantly explode in a burst of murderous frenzy is a fact that measures his horror, which paralyzed him where he stood. A civilized man in his position would have sought doubtful refuge in the conclusion that he was insane; it did not occur to the Cimmerian to doubt his senses. He knew he was face to face with a demon of the Elder World, and the realization robbed him of all his faculties except sight.

The trunk of the horror was lifted and quested about, the topaz eyes stared unseeingly, and Conan knew the monster was blind. With the thought came a thawing of his frozen nerves, and he began to back silently toward the door. But the creature heard. The sensitive trunk stretched toward him, and Conan's horror froze him again when the being spoke, in a strange, stammering voice that never changed its key or timbre. The Cimmerian knew that those jaws were never built or intended for human speech.

"Who is here? Have you come to torture me again, Yara? Will you never be done? Oh, Yag-kosha, is there no end to agony?"

Tears rolled from the sightless eyes, and Conan's gaze strayed to the limbs stretched on the marble couch. And he knew the monster would not rise to attack him. He knew the marks of the rack, and the searing brand of the flame, and tough souled as he was, he stood aghast at the ruined deformities which his reason told him had once been limbs as comely as his own. And suddenly all fear and repulsion went from him, to be replaced by a great pity. What this monster was, Conan could not know, but the evidences of its sufferings were so terrible and pathetic that a strange aching sadness came over the Cimmerian, he knew not why. He only felt that he was looking upon a cosmic tragedy, and he shrank with shame, as if the guilt of a whole race were laid upon him.

"I am not Yara," he said. "I am only a thief. I will not harm you."

"Come near that I may touch you," the creature faltered, and Conan came near unfearingly, his sword hanging forgotten in his hand. The sensitive trunk came out and groped over his face and shoulders, as a blind man gropes, and its touch was light as a girl's hand.

"You are not of Yara's race of devils," sighed the creature. "The clean, lean fierceness of the wastelands marks you. I know your people from of old, whom I knew by another name in the long, long ago when another world lifted its jeweled spires to the stars. There is blood on your fingers."

"A spider in the chamber above and a lion in the garden," muttered Conan. "You have slain a man too, this night," answered the other. "And there is death in the tower above. I feel; I know."

"Aye," muttered Conan. "The prince of all thieves lies there dead from the bite of a vermin."

"So—and so!" the strange inhuman voice rose in a sort of low chant. "A slaying in the tavern and a slaying on the roof—I know; I feel. And the third will make the magic of which not even Yara dreams—oh, magic of deliverance, green gods of Yag!"

Again tears fell as the tortured body was rocked to and fro in the grip of varied emotions. Conan looked on, bewildered.

Then the convulsions ceased; the soft, sightless eyes were turned toward the Cimmerian, the trunk beckoned.

"Oh man, listen," said the strange being. "I am foul and monstrous to you, am I not? Nay, do not answer; I know. But you would seem as strange to me, could I see you. There are many worlds besides this earth, and life takes many shapes. I am neither god nor demon, but flesh and blood like yourself, though the substance differ in part, and the form be cast in different mold.

"I am very old, oh man of the waste countries; long and long ago I came to this planet with others of my world, from the green planet Yag, which circles for ever in the outer fringe of this universe. We swept through space on mighty wings that drove us through the cosmos quicker than light, because we had warred with the kings of Yag and were defeated and outcast. But we could never return, for on earth our wings withered from our shoulders. Here we abode apart from earthly life. We fought the strange and terrible forms of life which then walked the earth, so that we became feared, and were not molested in the dim jungles of the east, where we had our abode.

"We saw men grow from the ape and build the shining cities of Valusia, Kamelia, Commoria, and their sisters. We saw them reel before the thrusts of the heathen Atlanteans and Picts and Lemurians. We saw the oceans rise and engulf Atlantis and Lemuria, and the isles of the Picts, and the shining cities of civilization. We saw the survivors of Pictdom and Atlantis build their stone age empires, and go down to ruin, locked in bloody wars. We saw the Picts sink into abysmal savagery, the Atlanteans into apedom again. We saw new savages drift southward in conquering waves from the arctic circle to build a new civilization, with new kingdoms called Nemedia, and Koth, and Aquilonia and their sisters. We saw your people rise under a new name from the jungles of the apes that had been Atlanteans. We saw the descendants of the Lemurians who had survived the cataclysm, rise again through savagery and ride westward, as Hyrkanians. And we saw this race of devils, survivors of the ancient civilization that was before Atlantis sank, come once more into culture and power—this accursed kingdom of Zamora.

"All this we saw, neither aiding nor hindering the immutable cosmic law, and one by one we died; for we of

35

Yag are not immortal, though our lives are as the lives of planets and constellations. At last I alone was left, dreaming of old times among the ruined temples of jungle-lost Khitai, worshipped as a god by an ancient yellow skinned race. Then came Yara, versed in dark knowledge handed down through the days of barbarism, since before Atlantis sank.

"First he sat at my feet and learned wisdom. But he was not satisfied with what I taught him, for it was white magic, and he wished evil lore, to enslave kings and glut a fiendish ambition. I would teach him none of the black secrets I had gained, through no wish of mine, through the eons.

"But his wisdom was deeper than I had guessed; with guile gotten among the dusky tombs of dark Stygia, he trapped me into divulging a secret I had not intended to bare; and turning my own power upon me, he enslaved me. Ah, gods of Yag, my cup has been bitter since that hour!

"He brought me up from the lost jungles of Khitai where the gray apes danced to the pipes of the yellow priests, and offerings of fruit and wine heaped my broken altars. No more was I a god to kindly jungle-folk—I was slave to a devil in human form."

Again tears stole from the unseeing eyes.

"He pent me in this tower which at his command I built for him in a single night. By fire and rack he mastered me, and by strange unearthly tortures you would not understand. In agony I would long ago have taken my own life, if I could.

But he kept me alive—mangled, blinded, and broken—to do his foul bidding. And for three hundred years I have done his bidding, from this marble couch, blackening my soul with cosmic sins, and staining my wisdom with crimes, because I had no other choice. Yet not all my ancient secrets has he wrested from me, and my last gift shall be the sorcery of the Blood and the Jewel.

"For I feel the end of time draw near. You are the hand of Fate. I beg of you, take the gem you will find on yonder altar."

Conan turned to the gold and ivory altar indicated, and took up a great round jewel, clear as crimson crystal; and he knew that this was the Heart of the Elephant.

"Now for the great magic, the mighty magic, such as earth has not seen before, and shall not see again, through a million million of millenniums. By my life-blood I conjure it, by blood born on the green breast of Yag, dreaming far-poised in the great blue vastness of Space.

"Take your sword, man, and cut out my heart; then squeeze it so that the blood will flow over the red stone. Then go you down these stairs and enter the ebony chamber where Yara sits wrapped in lotus-dreams of evil. Speak his name and he will awaken. Then lay this gem before him, and say, 'Yag-kosha gives you a last gift and a last enchantment.' Then get you from the tower quickly; fear not, your way shall be made clear. The life of man is not the life of Yag, nor is human death the death of Yag. Let me be free of this cage of broken blind flesh, and I will once more be Yogah of Yag, morning-crowned and shining, with wings to fly, and feet to dance, and eyes to see, and hands to break."

Uncertainly Conan approached, and Yag-kosha, or Yogah, as if sensing his uncertainty, indicated where he should strike. Conan set his teeth and drove the sword deep. Blood streamed over the blade and his hand, and the monster started convulsively, then lay back quite still. Sure that life had fled, at least life as he understood it, Conan set to work on his grisly task and quickly brought forth something that he felt must be the strange being's heart, though it differed curiously from any he had ever seen. Holding the still pulsing organ over the blazing jewel, he pressed it with both hands, and a rain of blood fell on the stone. To his surprise, it did not run off, but soaked into the gem, as water is absorbed by a sponge.

Holding the jewel gingerly, he went out of the fantastic chamber and came upon the silver steps. He did not look back; he instinctively felt that some sort of transmutation was taking place in the body on the marble couch, and he further felt that it was of a sort not to be witnessed by human eyes.

He closed the ivory door behind him and without hesitation descended the silver steps. It did not occur to him to ignore the instructions given him. He halted at an ebony door, in the center of which was a grinning silver skull, and pushed it open. He looked into a chamber of ebony and jet, and saw, on a black silken couch, a tall, spare form reclining. Yara the priest and sorcerer lay before him, his eyes open and dilated with the fumes of the yellow lotus, far-staring, as if fixed on gulfs and nighted abysses beyond human ken.

"Yara!" said Conan, like a judge pronouncing doom. "Awaken!"

The eyes cleared instantly and became cold and cruel as a vulture's. The tall silken-clad form lifted erect, and towered gauntly above the Cimmerian.

"Dog!" His hiss was like the voice of a cobra. "What do you here?"

Conan laid the jewel on the great ebony table.

"He who sent this gem bade me say, 'Yag-kosha gives a last gift and a last enchantment.'"

Yara recoiled, his dark face ashy. The jewel was no longer crystal-clear; its murky depths pulsed and throbbed, and curious smoky waves of changing color passed over its smooth surface. As if drawn hypnotically, Yara bent over the table and gripped the gem in his hands, staring into its shadowed depths, as if it were a magnet to draw the shuddering soul from his body. And as Conan looked, he thought that his eyes must be playing him tricks. For when Yara had risen up from his couch, the priest had seemed gigantically tall; yet now he saw that Yara's head would scarcely come to his shoulder. He blinked, puzzled, and for the first time that night, doubted his own senses. Then with a shock he realized that the priest was shrinking in stature— was growing smaller before his very gaze.

With a detached feeling he watched, as a man might watch a play; immersed in a feeling of overpowering unreality, the Cimmerian was no longer sure of his own identity; he only knew that he was looking upon the external evidences of the unseen play of vast Outer forces, beyond his understanding.

Now Yara was no bigger than a child; now like an infant he sprawled on the table, still grasping the jewel. And now the sorcerer suddenly realized his fate, and he sprang up, releasing the gem. But still he dwindled, and Conan saw a tiny, pigmy figure rushing wildly about the ebony table-top, waving tiny arms and shrieking in a voice that was like the squeak of an insect.

Now he had shrunk until the great jewel towered above him like a hill, and Conan saw him cover his eyes with his hands, as if to shield them from the glare, as he staggered about like a madman. Conan sensed that some unseen magnetic force was pulling Yara to the gem. Thrice he raced wildly about it in a narrowing circle, thrice he strove to turn and run out across the table; then with a scream that echoed faintly in the ears of the watcher, the priest threw up his arms and ran straight toward the blazing globe.

Bending close, Conan saw Yara clamber up the smooth, curving surface, impossibly, like a man climbing a glass mountain. Now the priest stood on the top, still with tossing arms, invoking what grisly names only the gods know. And suddenly he sank into the very heart of the jewel, as a man sinks into a sea, and Conan saw the smoky waves close over his head. Now he saw him in the crimson heart of the jewel, once more crystal-clear, as a man sees a scene far away, tiny with great distance. And into the heart came a green, shining winged figure with the body of a man and the head of an elephant—no longer blind or crippled. Yara threw up his arms and fled as a madman flees, and on his heels came the avenger. Then, like the bursting of a bubble, the great jewel vanished in a rainbow burst of iridescent gleams, and the ebony table-top lay bare and deserted—as bare, Conan somehow knew, as the marble couch in the chamber above, where the body of that strange transcosmic being called Yag-kosha and Yogah had lain.

The Cimmerian turned and fled from the chamber, down the silver stairs. So mazed was he that it did not occur to him to escape from the tower by the way he had entered it. Down that winding, shadowy silver well he ran, and came into a large chamber at the foot of the gleaming stairs. There he halted for an instant; he had come into the room of the soldiers. He saw the glitter of their silver corselets, the sheen of their jeweled sword-hilts. They sat slumped at the banquet board, their dusky plumes waving somberly above their drooping helmeted heads; they lay among their dice and fallen goblets on the wine-stained lapis-lazuli floor. And he knew that they were dead. The promise had been made, the word kept; whether sorcery or magic or the falling shadow of great green wings had stilled the revelry, Conan could not know, but his way had been made clear. And a silver door stood open, framed in the whiteness of dawn.

Into the waving green gardens came the Cimmerian, and as the dawn wind blew upon him with the cool fragrance of luxuriant growths, he started like a man waking from a dream. He turned back uncertainly, to stare at the cryptic tower he had just left. Was he bewitched and enchanted? Had he dreamed all that had seemed to have passed? As he looked he saw the gleaming tower sway against the crimson dawn, its jewel-crusted rim sparkling in the growing light, and crash into shining shards.